Would You Rather pirate Game

⚔ MAZE pirate Game is a classic maze (labyrinth) puzzle for kids and adults with fun tweaks and surprises!

⚔ In this game, you just swipe your the pen and guide the dot through the walls to find On the treasure!

⚔ ATTACK your Mateys' islands! Take their good stuff (and coins)! - it's a pirate's life, after all!

⚔ STEAL bonuses and prizes from other pirates! Take what your heart desires!

⚔ Yo-ho! Will become the richest Pirate King master of all?

⚔ Anything goes in the most pirate-tastic of multiplayer games and maze games!

⚔ Bonuses and Loot A-Plenty In This maze Island Adventure Game!

⚔ Find the only On the treasure out in tons of mazes (labyrinths) and become the king of the maze. Once you start, you'll be hooked. Try to play The Maze and I'm sure it will cause a mania for you!

The
CAT PIRATE
ANSWER

CAT PIRATE

1. Spyglass 2. Island 3. Treasure
4. Map 5. Hat 6. Dagger 7. Compass

Answer: pirates

The
CAT PIRATE

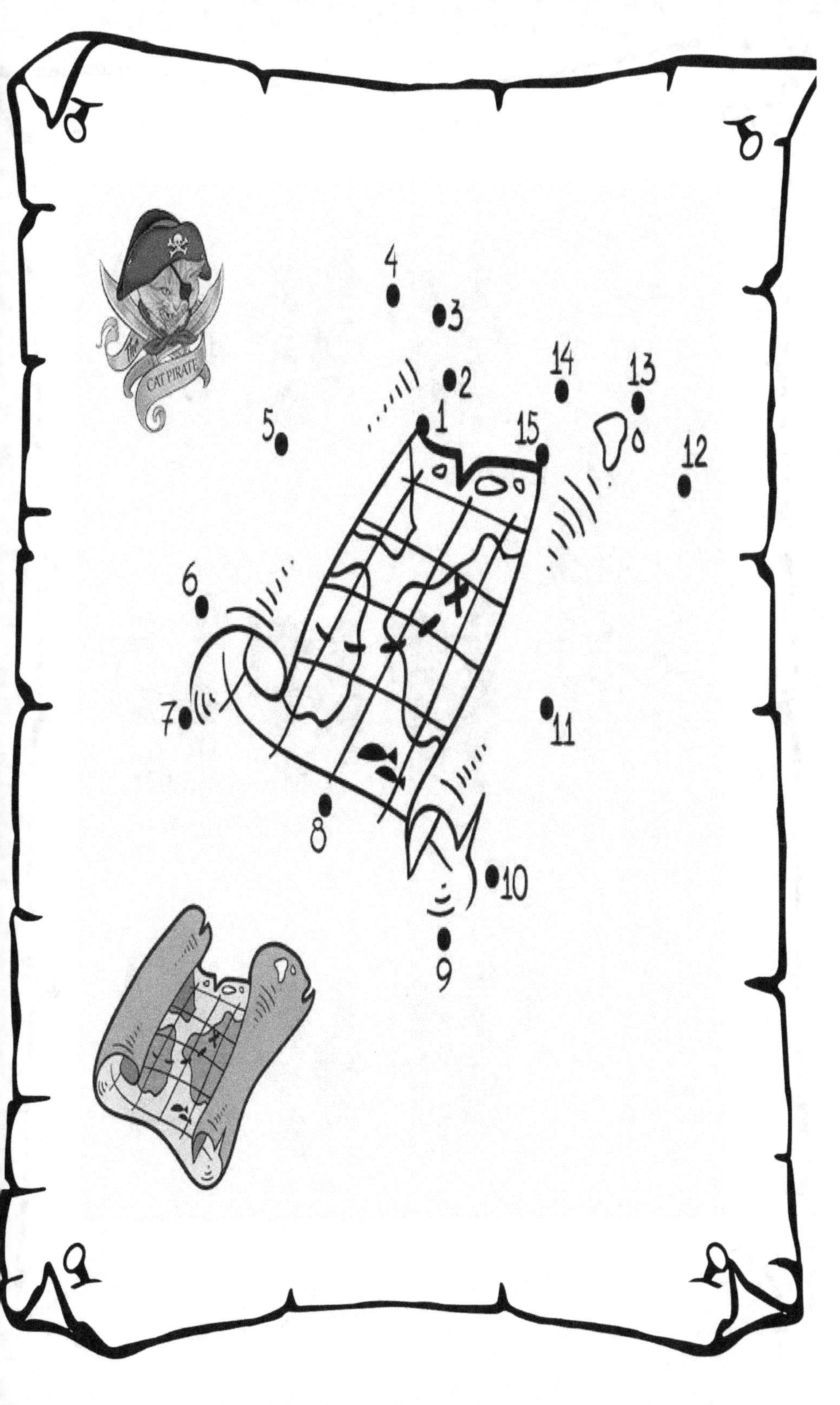
CAT PIRATE

ANSWER

A
B
C
D
E
CAPTROATE

CAT PIRATE

1
2
3

Which of these little pirates will succeed to reach to the treasure chest?

0 1 2 3 4 5 6 7 8 9 + −
10 11 12 13 14 15 16 17 18 19 20 =
0 1 2 3 4 5 6 7 8 9
= + + +

The
CAT PIRATE

FiNisH
1
2
3
START

The
CAT PIRATE

The CAT PIRATE
1
2
3
4
5
6
N W E S
TREASURE

BEACH FUN
The CAT PIRATE

Help the pirate
find the key to open
his treasure chest.

The CAT PIRATE

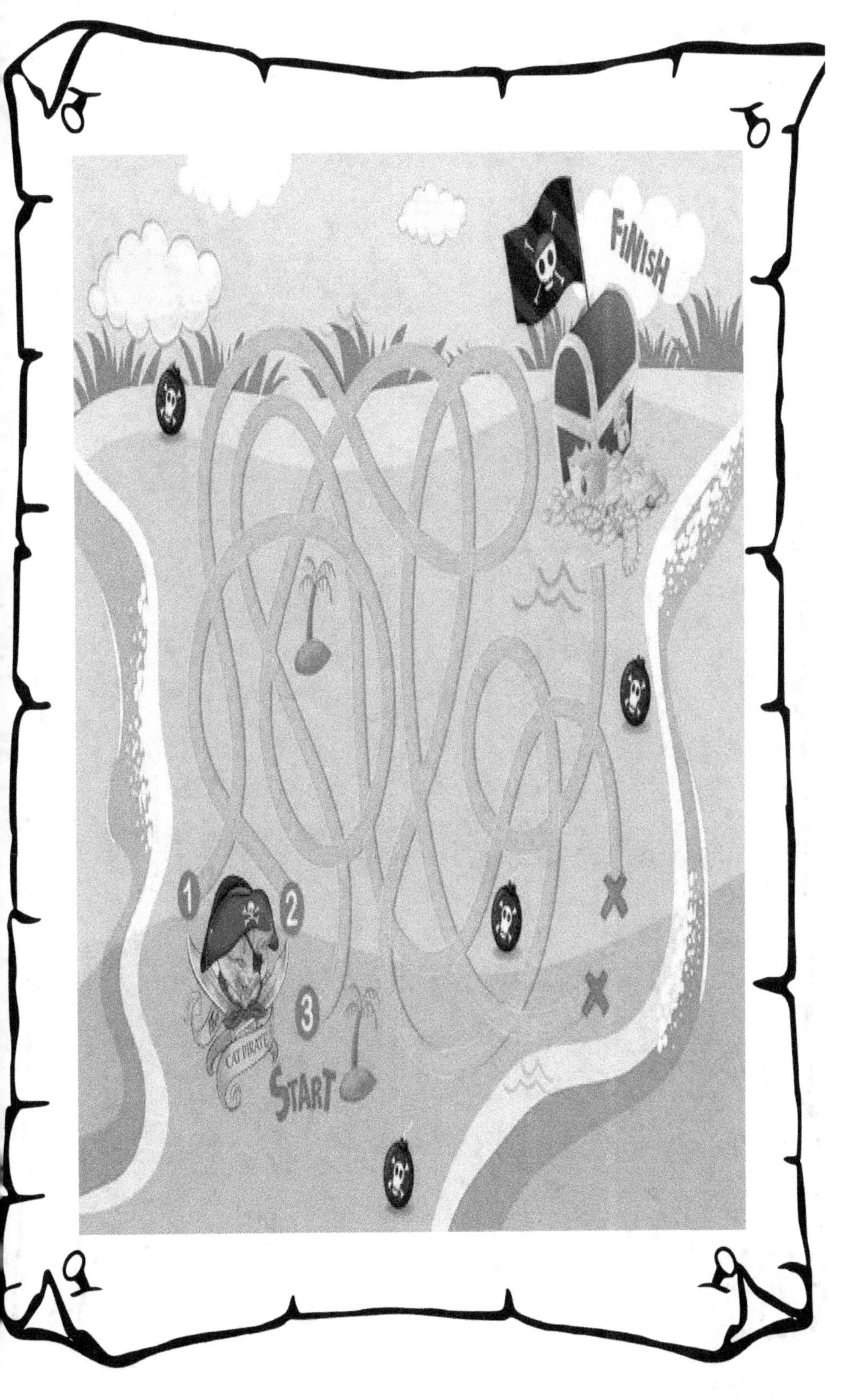

FINISH
1
2
3
CAT PIRATE
START

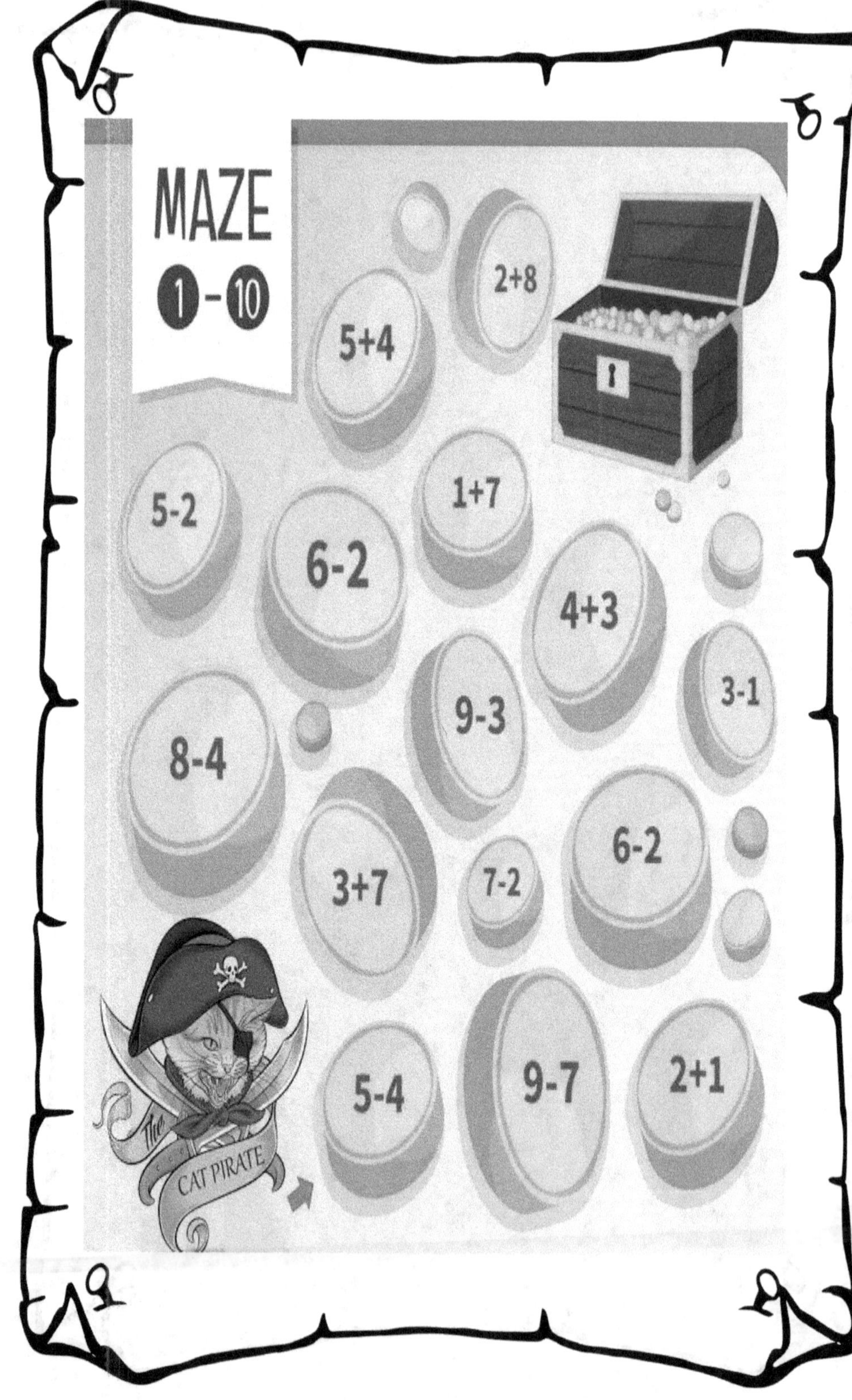

MAZE
1 – 10
2+8
5+4
5-2
1+7
6-2
4+3
3-1
9-3
8-4
6-2
3+7
7-2
5-4
9-7
2+1
The
CAT PIRATE

CAT PIRATE

Add the letters using the key and read the phrase
CAT PIRATE
PIRATE TREASURE
Answer: PIRATE TREASURE

CAT PIRATE

The
CAT PIRATE

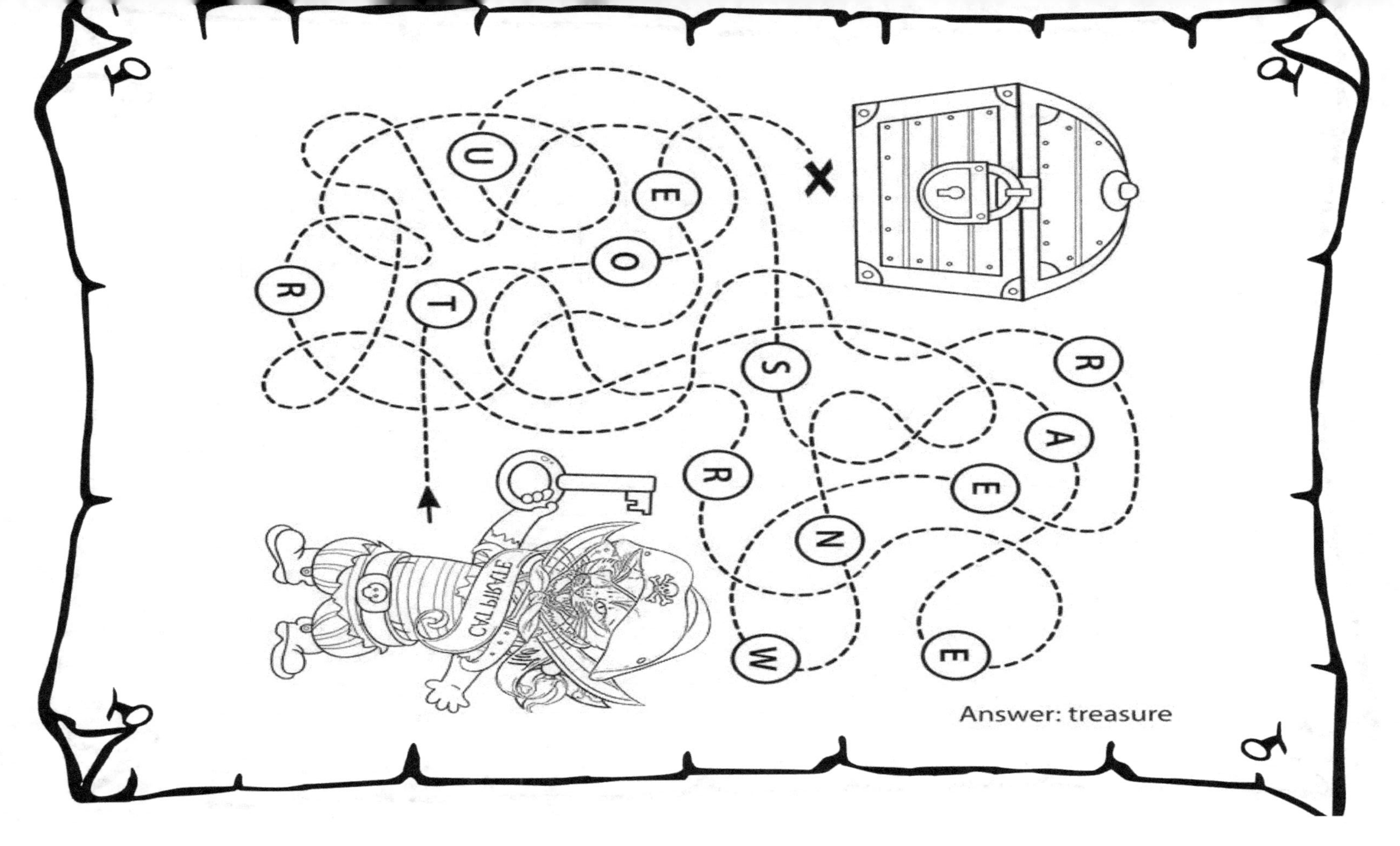
Answer: treasure

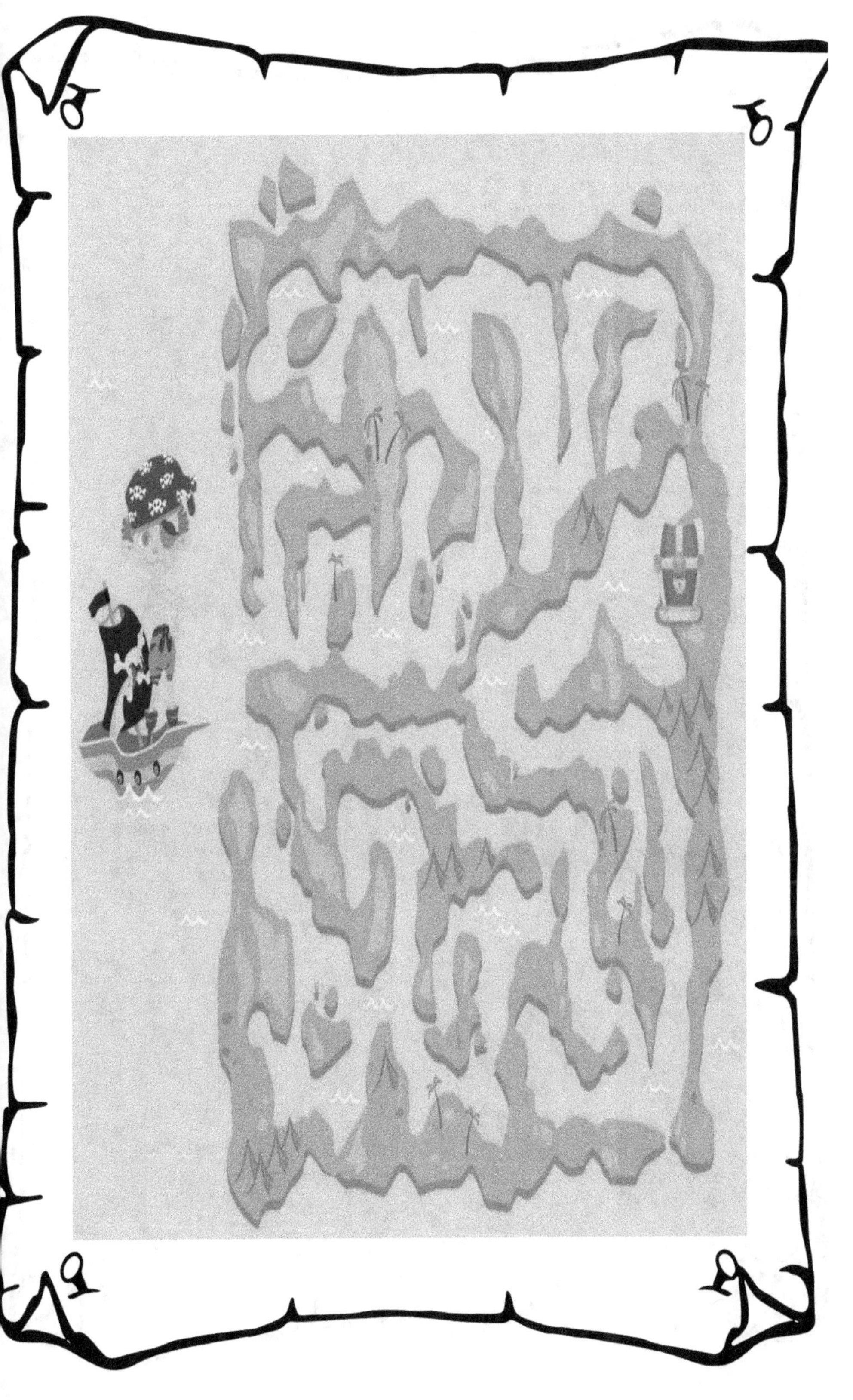

PIRATE TREASURE

HOTEL
CAT PIRATE

CAT PIRATE

MATCH CHESTS AND LOCKS BY SIZE

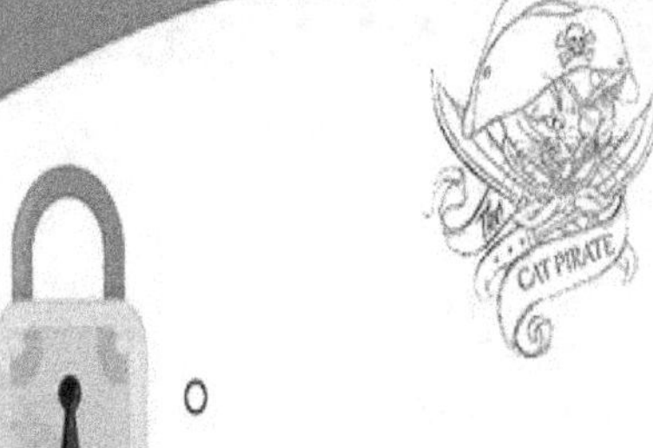

ANSWER:

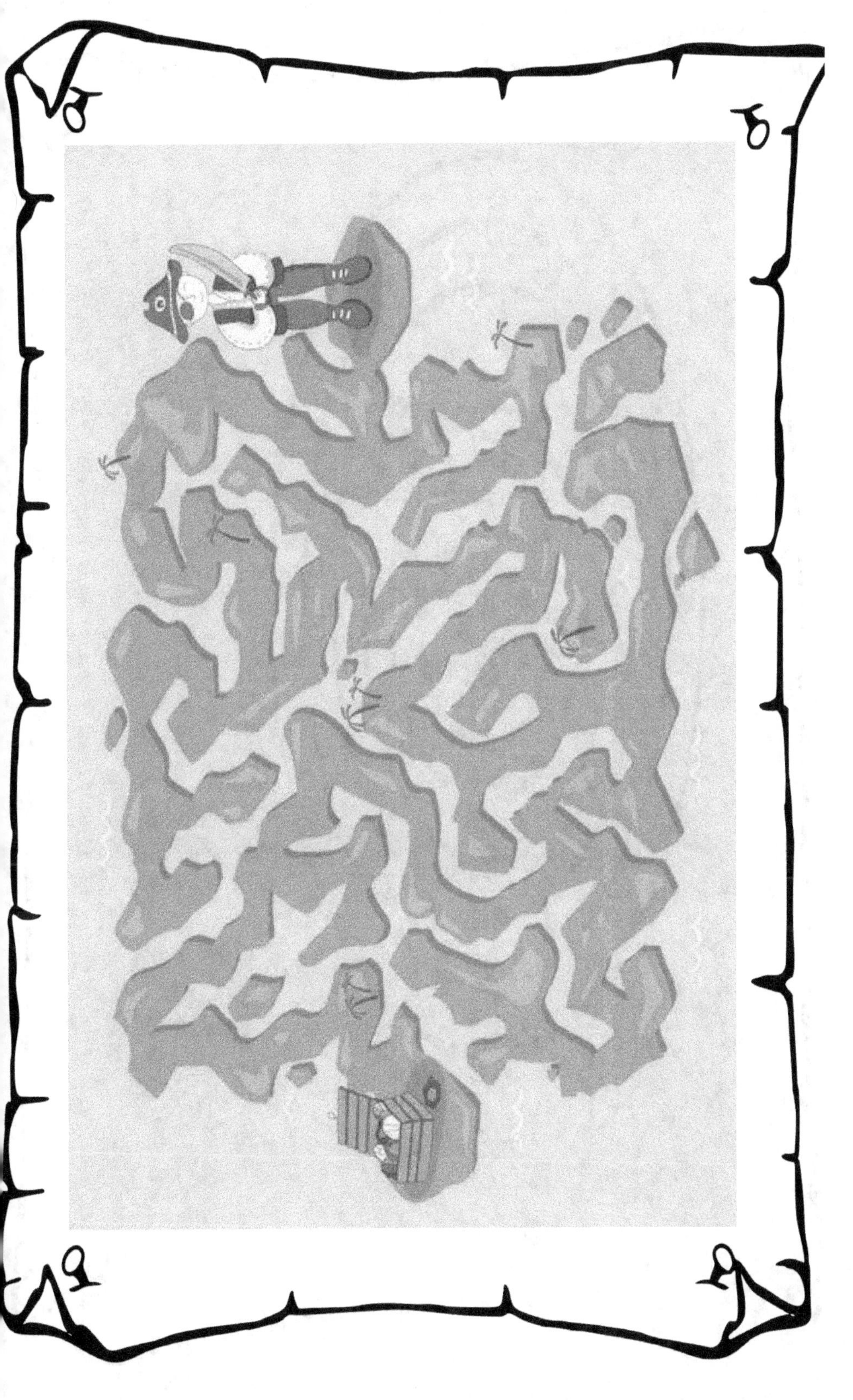

CAT PIRATE

CAT PIRATE

CAT PIRATE

CAT PIRATE

The
CAT PIRATE

The
CAT PIRATE

PA OLA NASCOST : _ _ _ _ _ _

C	M	O	N	E	T	E	A
O	M	A	P	P	A	L	O
R	E	L	A	P	O	M	R
S	V	O	D	B	A	A	O
A	A	S	A	I	L	R	S
R	N	I	P	R	E	E	E
I	C	A	S	T	V	I	T
S	E	N	O	N	N	A	C

CANNONE
CORSARI
ISOLA
MAPPA
MARE
MONETE
NAVE
SCIABOLA
SPADA
TESORO
VELA

Column clues

1	2	3	4	5	6	7	8	9	10	11	12	13	14	15
							3							
		2	2	2	2	2	1	2	2	2	2	2		
		3	1	1	1	2	1	2	1	1	1	3		
	6	1	1	1	1	3	1	3	1	1	1	1	6	
1	7	1	3	1	1	1	1	1	1	1	3	1	7	1

Row clues

			11
			13
	1	1	1
		1	1
	1	3	1
1	2	2	1
1	2	2	1
		1	1
			13
2	1	1	2
	1	3	1
		1	1
		3	3
1	1	1	1
			15

The CAT PIRATE

The
CAT PIRATE

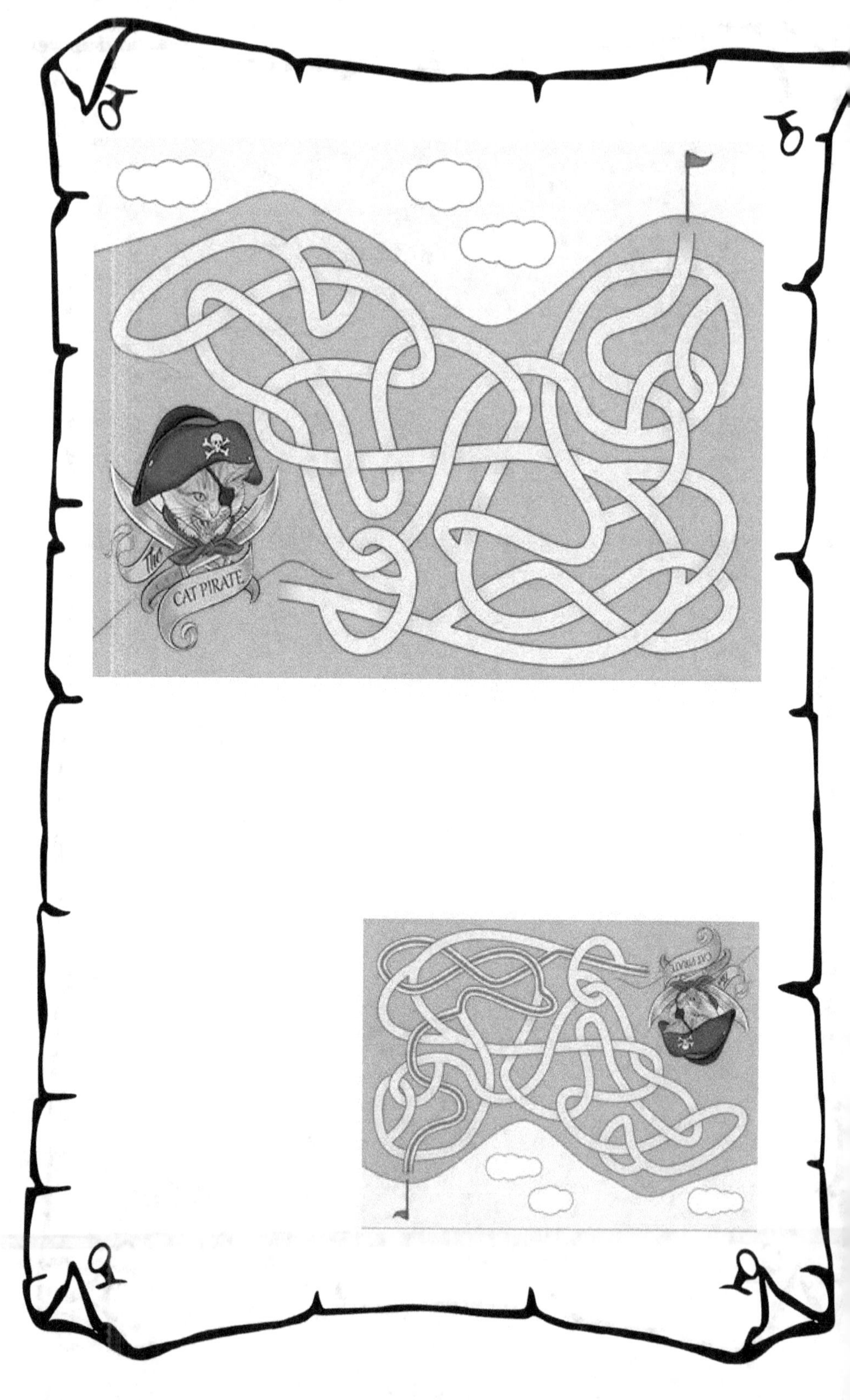
The
CAT PIRATE
CAT PIRATE

Finish
Start

The
CAT PIRATE
Hello

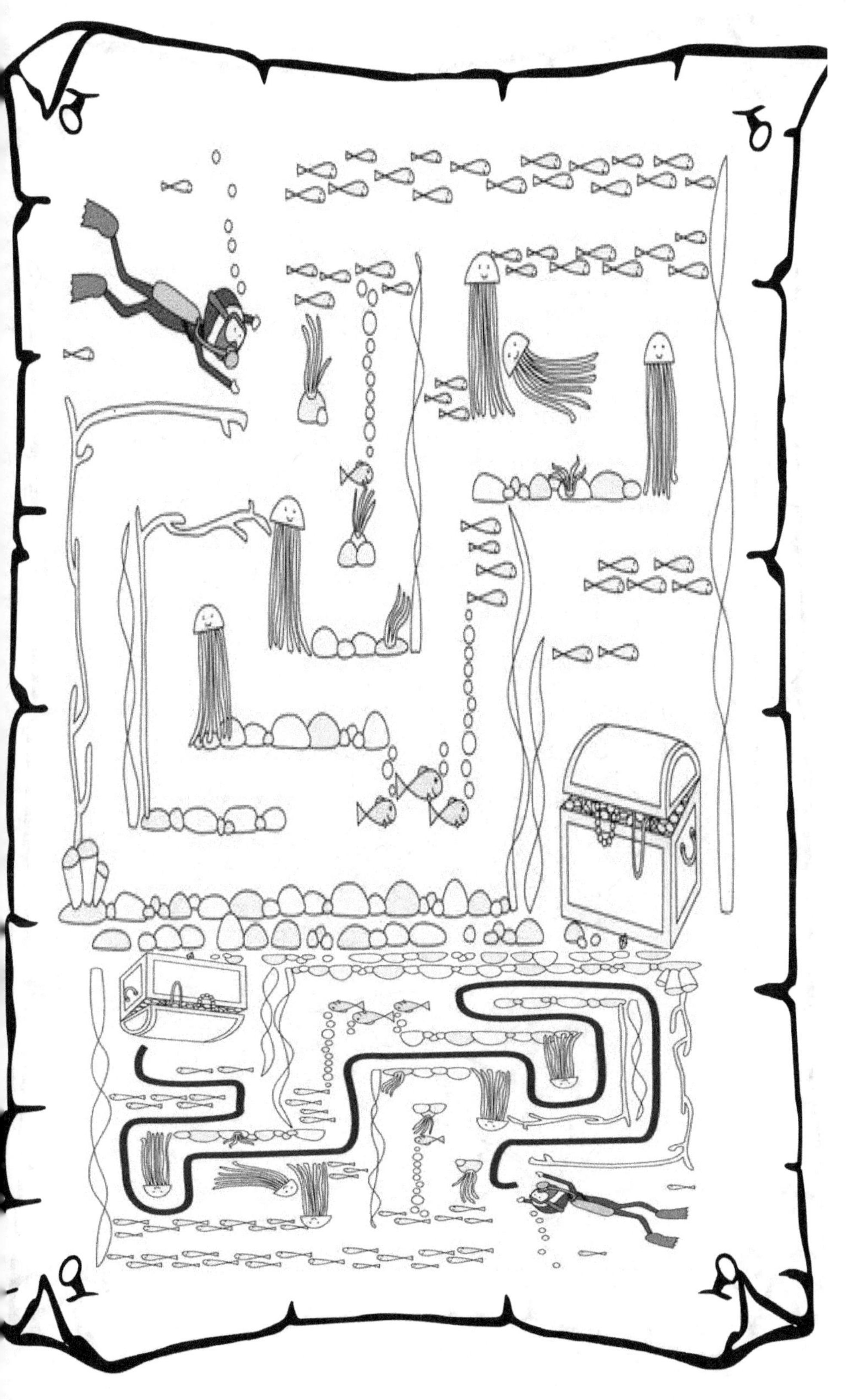

The
CAT PIRATE
NOTES

CAT PIRATE

CAT PIRATE

CAT PIRATE
NOTES

CAT PIRATE

Treasure Island Maze
Game with Pirate Supplies